BARTHOLOMEW
and
THE CHRIST CHILD

By Steve E. Upchurch

BARTHOLOMEW
and
THE CHRIST CHILD

Steve E. Upchurch, Author

Copyright ©2020 Steve E. Upchurch

Cover image used with permission from www.pixabay.com
Cover design and layout by Crystal Deeds

ISBN 978-1-7329962-9-8
Nook: 978-1-7345628-0-4
Kindle: 978-1-7345628-1-1

Set in Calibri
Printed in the United States of America

The views of this book are solely the views of Steve E. Upchurch. Parts of some of the stories have been fictionalized for entertainment value. The characters are fictional and for illustrative purposes only.

All scripture taken from the HOLY BIBLE, New King James Version
Copyright © 1982 by Thomas Nelson, Inc.

Table of Contents

INTRODUCTION

**Every person that has ever *truly* met Jesus Christ
has been changed...**

Mary and Joseph were demanded by Caesar Augustus to register for the census in Jerusalem. On their way through Bethlehem, as Mary was preparing to give birth, they stopped at the Bethlehem Inn.

This fictional story imagines how the life of a stable boy may have changed after his encounter with Mary and Joseph.

The stable boy chronicles, from his own perspective, the story of the birth of Jesus Christ and the aftermath, beginning from the age of fifteen, when he first meets Mary and Joseph, until he reaches the age of forty-eight.

CHAPTER ONE

My name is Bartholomew. I am currently forty-eight years old. However, this story starts thirty-three years ago when I had just turned fifteen. I hate to admit it, but I am still struggling to completely understand what happened at my father and mother's inn in Bethlehem.

Bethlehem Inn has been in our family for several generations. My grandfather grew up helping his father run the inn. My dad grew up helping my grandfather run the inn. Now I am helping my dad run the inn.

There were six of us kids. I was the oldest. Next in line were four girls. The oldest of my sisters is named Rachael, next in line is Rebecca, the third sister's name is Martha, and my youngest sister's name is Deborah, and then... there was Timothy. Timothy was the youngest. Being the youngest, he was the favorite of the entire family. It seemed like he was always in a good mood. When he laughed, his chubby, rose-colored cheeks bounced up and down, and his eyes glimmered with the most mischievous twinkle. Everyone spoiled him rotten!

Timothy was my sidekick. It was clear to see that, as his only brother, I was his hero. As soon as he could walk, everywhere I went, Timothy was right there... usually right in the way! However, it honestly didn't bother me one bit. I loved having him tag along.

Our family was a typical Jewish family. My mom and dad taught all of us kids, scriptures from the Torah, and we went to the synagogue on a regular basis. We were taught to obey the ten commandments, and we also went to the temple every year at Passover to offer up yearly sacrifices. On top of all of that, my parents were careful to faithfully give a tenth from the crops we harvested and a tenth of all profits from the inn.

Along with religion, one topic that frequently was discussed around the dinner table was politics and King Herod. King Herod was considered the king of Israel, and was the second son of Antipater the Idumaean, a high-ranking official in the Roman government. Herod's father was, by descent, an Edomite whose ancestors had converted to Judaism, which is what "qualified" him as our king.

My dad did not like him one bit! He thought he was a traitor to the Jewish people, always complaining that his rise to power was largely due to his father's relationship with Julius Caesar.

"He's only the King of Israel because his daddy is friends with Caesar," my dad would say frequently, with a snarl on his face.

When he would start ranting my mother would roll her eyes and try to change the subject. All of us kids thought it was funny.

With Israel under the control of Caesar and the Romans, we, as Jews, weren't considered slaves, but we were captive to the laws and control of the Roman government.

King Herod was known to willingly do Caesar's bidding, especially if it lined his pockets with gold and silver.

I remember once, when I was thirteen years old, King Herod actually had spent the night at our inn. At first, we thought it might be cool having the king stay at our inn, however, the first thing he did was demand that the rest of the inn be cleared of all clients. So, my dad had to go to each room and make people pack up and leave immediately. He was so mad he could hardly see straight!

I hid around the corner, listening as my dad tried to reason with Herod, but he wouldn't budge. "I don't want *'those kind of people'* here while I am here!" he demanded, with a haughty voice. It was all my dad could do to keep his mouth shut.

As soon as he was out of hearing range, I heard my father mutter, *"... you would be one of 'those kinds of people' if your daddy wasn't friends with Caesar!"*

Herod strutted around our inn, treating all of us like we were his own personal servants... demanding everything be exactly how he liked it... and speaking degradingly to all of us. He even made fun of little Timothy, and that made my blood boil!

"What an arrogant tyrant!!!" I thought.

He blatantly abused the power and prestige that came with being the king. He pranced around our inn in his royal robe, actually wearing the royal crown like he owned the place. On every finger of both hands were the most gawdy rings I had ever seen. UGGHH!!!!

My mom stayed as close to my dad as she could. I could tell that she was trying to keep him from saying something that would get him in trouble. Somehow, she succeeded in helping him keep his mouth shut.

Well, he kept it shut until the king left. Then he ranted non-stop for several weeks.

Outside of that, life was good. The inn provided a comfortable living for my parents, and all of us kids enjoyed the flow of interesting people that stopped by the inn.

Then came the day that changed everything.

I remember that day very well because it was my fifteenth birthday. My parents always made sure our birthdays were special, so I woke up excited to see how the day would unfold.

Timothy was just a few weeks from being two years old and was starting to talk in complete sentences. He was so funny! He couldn't pronounce his "r's" or "t's", so he called me *"Baa..folu..mew"*. Even though he didn't quite understand what birthdays were all about, he knew something special was going on, and was very excited on my behalf. He could tell it was a very special day for me.

I was the first one awake, so I excitedly knocked on my mom and dad's bedroom door, yelling for them to get up! On our birthdays my mom always fixed our favorite meals.

My Mom got out of bed, got dressed, and quickly pulled her hair back into a bun and made her way to the kitchen. We chit-chatted as she fixed my favorite breakfast. As soon as it was ready, she called everyone in to eat.

I was so happy!

Of course, everyone had to sing to me. Even though Timothy didn't know the words, he was trying his best to sing along with my sisters. It was wonderful!

"Go ahead and open your presents right now son, while we have the time," my dad said. "With so many people on the road traveling to Jerusalem we may not have time to celebrate later on. I'm sorry you're going to have to work so hard on your birthday."

"Aw, it's okay, dad," I replied. "I like it when we have a lot of people coming and going. It makes the day go by quicker!"

"Well, happy birthday anyway, son," he responded, with a huge smile on his face.

Because of the gift they got for me, I actually *felt* older. Instead of a toy, or something rather childish, mom and dad gave me my very own set of carpenter tools. It was *exactly* what I wanted!

"Thank you! Thank you! Thank you!" I shouted, hugging them both at the same time.

Picking up the hammer, and twirling it in his hand, my dad said, "I don't know much about carpentry, but I'll try to teach you what I know," with a big grin on his face.

Each of my sisters had created their own birthday cards, but my favorite card was the one they had helped Timothy make for me. I could tell they had held his chubby little hand in theirs as they helped him write his name on the card. He was so excited to give it to me.

I didn't realize it at the time, but that card from Timothy would become one of my most prized possessions that I would hold onto for many, many years.

After we finished eating, my dad placed his arm over my shoulders and took me on a walk around our property. As we slowly walked, he gave a long speech about how I was now a "young man", and as a "young man" I needed to start taking on more responsibilities at the inn. Part of those new responsibilities now included the feeding of all the livestock and maintaining the stables.

He went on and on about how important that job was. He talked about how the animals provided food, not only for us, but the animals were also a source of income for the entire family. Therefore, it was important that they were fed and watered on a regular basis.

I nodded and tried my best to pay attention to everything he said.

Even though that was thirty-three years ago, I remember that entire day like it was just yesterday.

My dad was right. Even though it was my birthday, it was still a workday, and a very busy workday at that. With so many people traveling on their way to Jerusalem to register for the census, there were people coming and going all day long.

However, it was still a wonderful day.

My dad was in a very good mood. Not only was he happy about it being my birthday, he was also very happy because the census was bringing more people into the inn than normal.

Every time things slowed down a little, my sisters and I would sneak out by the road and watch the parade of people on their way to Jerusalem. There were people on horses, people on donkeys... there were even people on camels. We just loved watching them as they made their way toward Jerusalem. Timothy liked sitting on my lap and waving at people as they went by.

That evening every room in the inn filled up quickly. We were out of rooms by the time the sun went down.

I was getting ready to gather up the eggs from our chickens when my dad stepped outside and shouted out my name. I came running as quickly as possible.

"Go clean out one of the stables as quickly as you can," he said.

CHAPTER TWO

"**W**hat's up?" I asked, in response to my dad's request to clean out a stable.

"Well, we have an emergency," he answered. "A young couple just showed up, and they're looking for a place to spend the night."

"But, we're out of rooms," I said.

"I know, but we *have* to find a place for this young couple," he replied, with a hint of panic in his voice. "The young lady is very, very, pregnant." he said. "In fact, she is already having labor pains and it's clear that she is going to give birth before the night's over!"

"Wow! But you're going to put them in a *stinky stable*???" I asked.

"Well, with all the rooms being taken," my dad replied, "it's either put them in a stable or she's going to have that baby in our front yard..."

"Okay... which stable do you want me to clean out for them?" I asked.

With a grin on his face, he replied, "You're a man now. I'll let you make that decision."

I quickly made the decision to move the sheep that were in one of the smaller stables into a larger stable with the other sheep. Then I grabbed a rake and shovel and raked up the hay and manure that was on the floor and shoveled it out behind the stable.

I then grabbed a fresh bale of hay and scattered it on the floor to make it smell and look as clean as I possibly could. The whole time Timothy was right there toddling at my feet and getting in the way.

I was so proud of the job I had done. The new hay on the floor actually made the stable quite presentable. It definitely made it *smell* better!

My father apologized over and over to the young couple, as he and my oldest sister, Rachael, brought Mary and Joseph out to the stable that I had prepared for them. "I'm so sorry we don't have any more rooms left," he was saying. "I've even moved all of my daughters into one bedroom so that an elderly couple could use one of our personal bedrooms."

To which my sister Rachael mumbled, *"Ya... I have sleep next to Deborah... it's like sleeping with a scared chicken..."*

My dad gave her his patented *"be quiet"* look.

"Oh, that's fine," Joseph replied. "We'll take anything you've got."

"Bartholomew," my dad said, looking at me as he entered the freshly cleaned stable, "this is Joseph and Mary." Then he looked around and smiled his approval at what I had done to fix it up.

"Joseph... Mary... this is my oldest son, Bartholomew, and my oldest daughter Rachael," he continued, with a proud look on his face, "and this curly headed, rug-rat is Timothy, my youngest son. If you need anything just call on Bartholomew. He is a fine young man, and he'll help you with anything you need."

My dad winked knowingly at me as he headed back to the inn, making me feel like he and I were now partners.

Mary and Joseph thanked me for cleaning out the stable, and Joseph started unloading their belongings from the back of their donkey.

I jumped in and helped them as much as I could. They were both so kind, I immediately liked them very much.

8

Joseph was so gentle as he helped Mary to the pile of hay I had gathered together for them to use for a bed. He took several blankets from their belongings and spread them out and helped Mary get as comfortable as she could.

Poor Mary looked absolutely miserable. Yet, at the same time, she had the most serene look on her face.

"Is there anything I can get for you? Some water... maybe some food?" I asked.

"Yes," Joseph answered. "We brought plenty of food with us, but if you don't mind, we sure could use some fresh water."

I took Timothy with me, and Rachel stayed with Mary, helping her as much as she could. When we brought the water, Joseph thanked me. Then he asked if we had an extra feeding trough or a manger available.

"What do you need a manger for?" I asked, with a quizzical look on my face.

"Well, we need a place to lay the baby when he is born, and I thought a manger would make a perfect crib," Joseph answered.

"We don't have an extra one, but we do have a stack of extra wood behind the stable. I would love to try to build one. I just got a set of carpenter tools for my birthday and I've been looking for something to build!" I said, with excitement in my voice.

Even though she was having labor pains, Mary was so kind to ask, "So, today is your birthday?"

"Yes, ma'am. I am fifteen years old today!" I said proudly.

"Well, happy birthday, Bartholomew!" She said with as much joy as she could muster. "Who knows… maybe our son will share your birthday," she added.

I looked at her with a quizzical look on my face. "How do you know it's going to be a boy?"

Rachael was curious. "Yah, how do you know it's not going to be a girl?"

She smiled at Joseph, and Joseph winked back at her and turned to me and said, "Trust me… we know!"

I was curious as to how they seemed to just *know* the child was going to be a boy.

Changing the subject Joseph asked, "So, do you know very much about carpentry?"

"Not much. I know how to build a fence and mend a hole in a stable wall. That's about it. My dad doesn't know much about building stuff, so it looks like I'm going to have to learn on my own."

Without taking a breath I continued, "I know my dad wants me to help him run the inn, which I'm happy to do, but I would really like to learn how to build furniture on the side."

The grin on Joseph's face got even bigger. "Well, Bartholomew, that's *exactly* what I do for a living," he responded.

"Seriously?" I asked, hardly believing my ears.

"Yes. I build furniture for a living. That's what my dad did for a living, and that's what his dad did for a living!"

He turned and checked on Mary. She finally looked more comfortable and, in less pain, now that she was able to get off of her feet and lay down.

"How far apart are your contractions?" Joseph asked gently.

"I'm pretty sure we have several hours to go," she answered.

"Why don't you rest for a little while," Joseph said softly. "And if you don't mind, I'm going to show this young man a few tricks of the carpenter trade."

Mary smiled her approval and responded, "You go right ahead. I'll be just fine."

"Is it okay if I stay here with you, Mary?" Rachael asked.

"Of course, dear. I would love the company," Mary responded with a warm smile.

"And I'll be right outside if you need me," Joseph said over his shoulder as he and I made our way out of the stable.

Watching Joseph's interaction with me, I think Mary was catching a glimpse of the kind of father Joseph was going to be to Jesus, because she had the most pleasant look of admiration on her face as we left.

"Go ahead. I'll be fine... I could use some girl talk anyway," she responded, grinning at Rachael.

I quickly ran and got my new tools, dragging Timothy with me all the way there and back.

I could hardly contain my joy at the thought of a *real* carpenter teaching me a few tricks of the trade.

I'll never forget how patient Joseph was as he showed me how to cut boards on an angle, and how to cut notches in the joints to make the joints stronger. He showed me how to drive nails at slightly different angles to also strengthen the joints of the manger we were building.

He even involved Timothy. "Here, Timothy, you are the official nail holder," he said, acting like it was the most important job ever.

Timothy's face lit up, and he did his best to not drop any of the nails.

"Measure twice and cut once," Joseph said emphatically. "If my dad told me that once, he told me a hundred times."

I had to admit, the manger that Joseph and I built together was much better than any of the rickety mangers my dad had built!

"Now *THAT*... is a manger!" I said with a proud look on my face, as I finished driving in the last nail.

Joseph reached out and shook my hand firmly, like I was his right-hand-man. "Great job, Bartholomew!" he said.

I'll never forget that moment.

He then bent over and shook Timothy's hand as well.

I thought to myself, *"this is a very special man! I sure would like to be like him when I grow up!"*

As we were carrying the manger into the stable, I asked, "What made you think of using a manger for a crib? That was a great idea. Have you ever built a manger to be used for a crib before?" I asked.

"No," Joseph replied, with a slight smile on his face.

"So, what made you think of using a manger this time?" I questioned again.

"I don't know. It's like it just made sense."

I filled the manger with fresh hay, and took what looked like an extra blanket, and folded it and placed it over the hay.

I didn't realize at that moment, just how important that manger would be within a matter of hours!

When I turned and looked at Mary, I could hardly believe my eyes. Rachael was rubbing her feet!!!

Apparently, the surprise was on my face because Rachael spoke up and said, "Hey, she deserves this... she's about to give birth and has been riding a donkey for God only knows how long!"

"Hey," I said right back at her, "I don't have a problem with it. It's just that I've never, ever, seen you do something like this!"

"Hey..." Mary interrupted, with a big smile on her face... "let me in on this! This may be the best present anyone has ever given me!"

We all laughed. There was such a wonderful feeling there inside that lowly stable!

But then Mary suddenly winced in pain.

"Okay guys," Joseph said, "If you don't mind, it looks like it's time for a little privacy."

We knew what he meant, so I grabbed Timothy by the hand and said, "It's getting late anyway. And I need to take Timothy back to the house. But if you guys need anything feel free to come and get me."

They both grinned and waved as Rachael and I escorted Timothy out of the stable, and back to the inn.

However, as soon as we delivered Timothy back to my mom I quietly returned and stood outside of the stable. I couldn't explain it... I was just *drawn* to what was happening.

It wasn't just that a baby was getting ready to be born, I had experienced the excitement of someone having a baby with the birth of several of my siblings. It was something else. It was like there was something in the air. An *expectation* of something big that was getting ready to happen.

CHAPTER THREE

I stayed far enough away from the stable that I couldn't see what was going on and Mary and Joseph had their privacy... but close enough that I could hear everything that was going on inside the stable. I had to admit the painful sounds that Mary was making were quite alarming!

There were several times I put my hands over my ears to muffle her cries of pain. All the while Joseph kept talking to her in the most calm and reassuring voice I had ever heard.

Then... everything grew quiet.

Until the silence was broken by the sound of a baby crying!!!!

"He's here!" Joseph exclaimed. *"He's here! And He is **wonderful**!"*

"Of course, He is," Mary said softly. "That's exactly what the prophet Isaiah said about Him... that He would be called 'wonderful'."

I listened, with a big smile on my face, as they went on and on bragging about how beautiful Jesus was, and talking about how tiny His little fingers and toes were.

Then Joseph said, "Here, Mary, hold your Son, as I wash Him off."

I listened intently to the sounds of Joseph taking care of Jesus. Then he gently took care of Mary.

When it sounded like they were settled down I quietly knocked on the stable gate.

"Hey guys, is it okay if I come in?" I whispered.

"Of course, you can," Mary responded with a twinkle in her voice.

What an unbelievable sight! Mary looked absolutely heavenly laying there against Joseph, as Joseph had his arms wrapped around Mary. The sight of little baby Jesus wrapped tightly in swaddling clothes and snuggled into Mary's arms was such a beautiful picture.

"You guys sure do make a beautiful family," I said softly.

"Awww..." Mary responded, with a lovely smile on her face, and tear quickly appearing in her eyes. "That is such a precious thing to say!"

"Joseph is right," she added. "You *are* a special young man!"

"And I can already tell that you are going to be a special mom!" I answered.

We had such a very special moment, as we sat quietly adoring baby Jesus.

Finally, she broke the silence. "Would you like to see Him?" Mary proudly asked, pulling the blanket away from Jesus' small face.

"Sure!" I answered. "I'm the oldest in our family, so I'm used to being around babies."

Mary uncovered His face, and I knelt there in the hay looking with great curiosity at this newborn baby. It was like there was a radiant glow there in the stable!

"May I touch Him?" I asked.

"Of course, you can," Mary answered, with a grin on her face.

I slowly reached out my hand to stroke His tiny, perfectly shaped fingers.

When I did… Jesus unexpectedly grabbed my finger! I felt something quite peculiar. It was like a warmth started at my finger in His grasp and spread throughout my entire body.

I looked up at Mary and Joseph, and they both had the biggest grins on their faces. It was like they couldn't stop smiling!

And, I knew… somehow, I just knew… I was in the presence of someone very, very special.

Then, baby Jesus began to cry.

"What's wrong?" I asked. "I didn't do anything wrong, did I?"

"No," Joseph said, "You didn't do anything wrong." But then with a slight grin, he nodded his head toward the gate and added, "But if you don't mind giving us some privacy, I think it's time for Jesus to eat."

I squinted my eyes, and looked at Joseph, not quite understanding what he meant at first. Then, realizing what he was saying about Jesus needing to eat, I quickly apologized and stumbled out of the stable, feeling my ears turning beet red!

I heard them laughing quietly as I made my way back to the Inn.

However, I couldn't help but feel a little bit proud of myself when I overheard Joseph say, *"That sure is a fine young man!"*

"He most certainly is!" Mary added.

CHAPTER FOUR

"**A**re they doing okay?" my dad asked as I entered the house.

"Yes. And the baby is here!" I answered excitedly.

"Is it a boy or a girl?" my mom asked.

"It's a baby boy," I responded.

"Oh my," she said, "I can't wait to go see Him!"

"Well, you might want to wait a few minutes. It's supper time for little Jesus."

"*Jesus*?" my dad asked.

"Yes. They named him Jesus."

"Hmmm… I like that name," my mom responded with a big smile on her face. "Yes… I like that name very much!"

"Mom, have you ever had a weird feeling about something?" I asked.

"A weird feeling? What do you mean?"

"I'm not sure. I was kneeling in front of Mary and Joseph, and they let me touch Jesus. When I did, He grabbed my finger. And there was something about His touch that I can't explain. It was… different. It was like something powerful went through my whole body!"

"I think I know what you mean. Once, before any of you kids were born, your father and I went into Jerusalem during Passover. We were there when the goats were being offered up for the yearly sin sacrifice. I was in the Women's Court of the Temple, which was as far as I was allowed to go. On that particular day a slight breeze was carrying the fragrance from the burning incense right to where we were standing."

"You could actually smell it?" I asked, with amazement in my voice. I knew the importance of Passover, and the importance of a yearly sin sacrifice. "You were close enough to smell the incense?"

"Yes. On one hand it was wonderful, knowing what it signified. On the other hand, it was humbling because I hated knowing that just a few feet away an animal was losing its life for my sin."

"Was it bad?" I asked.

"I'll never forget the sound," she answered. "The sound that poor goat made just broke my heart. I started crying, but it was at that exact moment I caught the sweet scent of the incense burning. It was like you said, it was 'weird'. It was sad and beautiful at the same time!"

I saw tears in my mother's eyes and realized just how emotional the experience had been.

She reached out and pulled me close to her in a warm embrace.

"Thanks, mom," I mumbled as she squeezed my face against her shoulder.

CHAPTER FIVE

Later on that night, just as I was drifting off to sleep, I heard what sounded like a crowd of people approaching the inn. At first, I thought it might be late comers looking for a room, but something didn't quite sound right, so I got up to go check it out.

When I stepped outside, all I could see was the silhouette of several men walking slowly in the shadows. I don't mind telling you, I was a little scared.

"What are you men doing snooping around here in the middle of the night?" I asked using my gruffest voice, in case they were troublemakers.

Out of the shadows, an older, gray headed man stepped forward. "We're sorry. We're not trying to cause any problems."

Again, trying to sound older than my fifteen-year-old voice actually was, I responded, "What are you men doing here? All of our rooms are taken."

"Oh, we're not here looking for a room. We're actually looking for some*one*!"

"If you're looking for my father you need to come back at a decent hour. We usually get up at dawn," I replied, and turned to go back inside the house.

"No, we're not here to see your father. We're here on a *special mission*."

Now he had my undivided attention. "A *special mission*? What kind of *special mission*?"

Then I saw the kindness in his eyes.

"A *mission* from God," he answered, with great wisdom in his voice.

"A *mission* from God? Are you teasing me?"

"No," the old man answered. "We are on a mission from God. Now... I have a very, very odd question I need to ask you."

I backed away from him. "What do you want to know?" I asked, with a little bit of suspicion in my voice.

Even more kindness appeared in the old man's eyes, and a big smile appeared on his wrinkled, dirty face. "Is there any chance a baby was born here tonight?" he asked cautiously.

"Yessss???" ... I answered, with a question in my voice, finding it strange that he would know such a thing.

"Is that baby a boy?" he added, as the smile got a little bigger.

"Yes. Why are you asking such peculiar questions?"

Ignoring my question, he continued, "And, is there any chance that baby is *wrapped in swaddling clothes*?"

With raised eyebrows, and eyes wide-open I responded, "Yes of course, everyone would know that... *but why are you asking?*" I added with even more of a question in my voice.

Ignoring my question again, he asked yet another question. "And is the baby *lying in a manger*?"

"Yes, but how in the world could you possibly KNOW THAT?" I responded, this time more emphatically.

He didn't respond, and instead grinned from ear to ear.
22

I was starting to freak out a little bit. "I'm so confused, please explain, *HOW COULD YOU POSSIBLY KNOW THESE THINGS???*"

He grinned really big, and now I could see that a few of his teeth were missing. Throwing his head back and laughing as hard as he could, he shouted, *"AN ANGEL TOLD US!!!"*

"An angel told you?" I asked. *"A real angel told you?"*

"Yes. It appeared in the sky while we were out watching over our sheep and told us to come here to find a baby boy!"

I squinted my eyes, looking at the old shepherd closely and asked, "Okay... are you guys *DRUNK*?"

Every one of the shepherds threw their heads back and burst out laughing as loudly as they could.

"No... we're not drunk," The old shepherd responded, showing his toothless grin again, and wiping tears of laughter from his eyes with the back of his weathered hand.

"Seriously..." he continued, "an angel told us to come here. The angel said that if we came, we would find a baby boy wrapped in swaddling clothes and lying in a manger!"

"Those were the angel's *exact* words?" I asked.

"Yes. That is *exactly* what the angel said!"

"Well... you are in luck," I responded. "It just so happened a baby boy *was* born here tonight... and He *is* wrapped in swaddling clothes... and He *is* lying in a manger."

"Well, no time to waste! Please, take us to Him" the old shepherd shouted... *"He is CHRIST THE LORD!"*

They were in such a hurry to see the baby that they almost knocked me down rushing to get to the stable, but as soon as they got near the stable each one of them stopped abruptly.

I watched them cautiously, as they slowly removed the shepherd's wrappings from around their heads, and quietly and reverently approached the stable opening.

Knocking gently on the stable gate, the old shepherd, with his bearded chin bowed so low it was touching his chest, asked quietly, "May we come in?"

Even though they smelled like dirt, sweat and sheep... even though their clothes were worn and ragged... and even though they were nothing but uneducated shepherds... I watched and listened in amazement as Mary and Joseph welcomed these lowly men into the stable with open arms.

As I continued watching, I couldn't help but feel like I was standing in the most holy of places, as each and every one of them knelt to their knees and bowed their heads until their faces touched the straw I had scattered on the stable floor.

Rocking back and forth, with tears streaming down their dust covered faces they began to softly repeat what they said the angel had told them. Over and over... increasing in volume each time they said it, they repeated...

"Glory to God in the Highest...
And on earth... peace... and goodwill toward men!"

"Glory to God in the Highest...
And on earth... peace... and goodwill toward men!"

Over and over they repeated it, as they lifted their hands, while on bended knees in front of baby Jesus.

I watched in amazement as they unashamedly worshipped Him!

Then, as if obeying an unspoken command, in unison they stopped, and knelt in silence.

I had that *weird* feeling again. Something very special was happening in the stable behind the Bethlehem Inn.

I'll never forget how silent the night was. It was as if the whole world stood still. It was as if all of creation was bowing in awe with them.

"WHO IS THIS BABY???" I wondered to myself as I stood there watching this amazing scene unfold before me.

Eventually the shepherds got to their feet.

Then the old, gray headed shepherd introduced each of those that were there with him. Two of them were his sons, and the youngest was his grandson.

Now that they were fully visible, in the glow from the candles, I could see that the grandson was about my age. So, the next time he looked in my direction I motioned to him to step outside with me.

"What's your name?" I asked.

"Matthew," He responded. "What is your name?"

"My name is Bartholomew. How old are you, Matthew?"

"I am fifteen. My birthday was about a month ago."

I could hardly believe it. "Well, happy birthday! Guess what? I just turned fifteen today!"

Matthew grinned, and said, "Well, happy birthday to you!"

I leaned into Matthew and lowered my voice. "Did everything happen, with the angel and all that stuff, the way your grandpa said it did?" I asked.

"Yep. It sure did. And I don't mind telling you, it about scared me to death!"

Matthew went through the entire story that his grandfather had told, and it matched exactly what he had said.

Then, we talked about our families, and made small talk. I also found out we both had little brothers. I told him all about Timothy, and he told me all about his little brother, named Jonathon.

We shared several stories about the funny things our little brothers had done, and how they were our "little buddies".

After a few minutes of laughter, we returned to the stable to see what was going on with the other shepherds, and Mary, Joseph and Jesus.

Matthew's grandfather was telling Mary and Joseph how the angel appeared to them and announced the birth of Jesus.

"What exactly did the angel say?" Joseph was asking.

The old shepherd again showed his toothless grin. "Well, first of all, he about scared us to death. There we were, gathered around the fire, most of us were about half asleep... and suddenly the glory of the Lord shone down all around us! Matthew, my grandson over there, actually jumped up and took off running!"

I looked at Matthew, and he was nodding his head in agreement, with a sheepish grin on his face.

"Hey, you guys looked pretty scared yourselves," he inserted.

The account of the story was clearly very funny to the shepherds as they burst out laughing and shoved Matthew around a little bit, slapping him on the back.

"Anyway," the old shepherd continued, "The first thing the angel told us was not to be afraid. He said he was bringing good news that will cause great joy for all the people. He said that today, in the town of David, a Savior had been born, and He was the Messiah, the Lord."

Joseph and Mary were clearly overjoyed by the story the old shepherd was telling. "An angel actually told you guys that our Jesus is the Messiah?" Joseph asked.

"Yes, but that's not all," the old man responded. "The angel also gave us very specific instructions on what to look for. He said, 'This will be a sign to you. You will find a baby wrapped in swaddling cloths and lying in a manger'."

My mouth dropped open!
Joseph's mouth dropped open!
Mary's mouth dropped open!

I'll never forget the look on Mary and Joseph's faces. The only way I can describe it is a look of calm reassurance. It was like the more the shepherds described what had happened, the more it confirmed something they already knew.

I could tell that the shepherds didn't really want to leave, but eventually I could see they felt like they had overstayed their welcome, and they decided it was time to go.

As they left it was like they had been transformed into young men. There was joy in their eyes, a dance in their feet, and they were laughing... shouting... and praising and glorifying God!

I stood there watching the shepherds as they disappeared back into the shadows of the night.

I really hated seeing them go.

Suddenly, out of the corner of my eye I saw a light appear in my Dad's bedroom.

"What in the world is all that racket?" my dad asked, rubbing his sleepy eyes as he came stumbling out the front door with a lit candle in his hand.

"It's okay." I replied with a knowing smile on my face. "I'll tell you all about it in the morning."

CHAPTER SIX

"**Y**our eyes look awful," my mom said as I walked into the kitchen the next morning. "What time did you go to sleep last night?"

I ignored her question and instead excitedly began telling her, dad and my sisters what happened the night before.

By the time I finished telling them all about the shepherds and their special mission, the angels scaring them to death, and the specific instructions the angel gave them, they were on the edge of their seats.

Everyone was in such a hurry to go see Jesus for themselves they could hardly finish their breakfast.

As we approached the stable, a crowd was already gathering around, as those who were staying at the inn were hearing about the newborn baby, and the middle of the night visitors.

What amazed me the most was how respectful and reverent everyone was! It was as if everyone just *knew* something important had happened.

Mary and Joseph were so accommodating. They allowed every single person that wanted to see baby Jesus to do so. It was as if they knew Jesus didn't belong to just them. They knew that He belonged to everyone. He belonged to the entire world!

However, I noticed that Joseph kept a close watch over Mary to make sure she wasn't overwhelmed with visitors.

After an hour or so, everyone realized Mary needed some privacy, so they left without having to be told to do so.

Later on, that day I heard one of my sisters hollering as loud as she could, *"Come quick... come quick everyone... it looks like there are several Maji coming down the road!"*

We all ran out to see who it was. It wasn't very often that important rich people traveled the back roads of Bethlehem.

We watched as they got closer and closer.

"Who is it? Who is it?" my oldest sister asked repeatedly, jumping up and down with excitement.

We didn't know who they were, but we could tell that whoever they were, they were very important and very wealthy. They were dressed in the finest of robes and as they got closer, we could see that their camels were loaded down with all kinds of expensive things.

I ran out closer to the road, waving at them and expecting them to ride on by, but to my amazement they turned and steered their camels up to our Inn.

My sisters and I gathered around them, not believing they were actually stopping at our inn.

My father came running over to them as quickly as he could. I could see the dollar bill signs in my dad's eyes!

Using his most dignified voice my dad said, *"Welcome... Welcome... Welcome to Bethlehem Inn,"* as he bowed as a sign of respect. *"How can I be of assistance to you?"*

"Thank you for such a warm welcome," the lead Maji said. "We have been traveling for several months, and a warm, soft bed sure does sound wonderful."

"Do you mind if I ask what brings you to this part of the country?" my dad asked.

"This may sound strange," The lead Maji responded again, "but we are wise men from the East, and we're followers of the prophecies of Isaiah and Jeremiah. We believe that a very special baby has been born very, very close to where we are standing."

My entire family looked at each other, once again with our mouths hanging open.

"Why do you believe that?" My dad asked, with his eyes wide open in amazement.

"Again, this may sound a little odd... but we have been following a star that appeared about 3 months ago... and that star has led us **right here*!"*

I interrupted, "You have been following *WHAT*?"

The Maji smiled brightly and repeated, "We have been following a star."

"A star in the sky?" I asked.

His grin got bigger, "I know it sounds crazy, but yes, we have been following a star in the sky!"

I was still trying to figure this out. "And... this star was different than all of the other stars?"

By now all of the Maji had huge grins on their faces.

"YES!" They all answered in unison.

"Well... come on guys! Hop down off those camels and follow me. *I know exactly who you're looking for*!"

"You do? How do you know that?" the lead Maji said, as he tapped his camel with his foot and the camel bowed to its knees so he could dismount.

"Well… it just so happens you're not the first ones to come looking for the *Christ Child*!" I responded.

"The *Christ Child*?" One of the other Maji asked, as the rest of the camels were now bowing to their knees to let their riders down.

"Yes. That is what He is being called," I answered.

"So, He is REALLY HERE?" he asked with overwhelming emotion in his voice.

"Yes. He sure is. He's in one of our stables with His mom and Dad," I said excitedly.

"He's in a *STABLE*? What in the world is He doing in a *STABLE*? Don't you realize He is the King?"

"The KING?" my dad shouted. "The King of who?"

"The KING OF THE JEWS!"

I thought my dad was going to pass out. I could see the wheels turning in his head at the thought of King Herod no longer being our king, so I carried on with the conversation.

"He's in a stable because all of our rooms were full, and Mary, the mother, was in labor when they got here so we had to put them in the only place available, which was a stable."

"Hurry up and take us to Him!" The lead Maji exclaimed. Turning to the other wise men he added, "and don't forget the gifts!"

"Do you guys need some help?" I asked.

"Sure. You look young and strong. Grab that biggest gift right there," he responded, pointing to the fanciest box of the bunch.

When I picked it up it was all I could do to carry it.

Grunting, I asked, "What in the world is in here?"

"Gold!"

"Gold???" my dad questioned. "Who is it for?"

"It's for *the baby*!"

My dad turned and looked at my mom and mouthed quietly... *"The baby?"*

My mom quietly mouthed back... *"I know... and we didn't get Him anything!"*

I couldn't help but grin.

By now there was no hiding the fact that something really, really big was happening in our lowly stable. Every person in the Inn was now following us, and even some of our neighbors were making their way over to see what was going on as I led the Maji to the stable where baby Jesus lay.

I thought Maji were supposed to act reserved and dignified, but that was definitely not the case with these wise men. I have never seen such dignified men so excited. As they made their way to the stable, they reminded me of little boys on their way to a party. They were *rejoicing with exceeding great joy!*

They had the very same response the Shepherds had. As soon as they saw Jesus they immediately fell to their knees in reverence, and began to worship Him, bowing so low that their faces touched the hay on the manger floor.

Everyone watched in amazement as these educated, wealthy Maji humbled themselves and bowed down, again and again.

The only time I had seen anything even close to this kind of behavior was when Caesar came to Jerusalem, and everyone bowed as his royal chariot drove past.

However, this was different. These wise men weren't bowing because they feared what would happen if they didn't bow down, like those bowing to Caesar. They were bowing the same way the shepherds had bowed... they were filled with awe and wonder!

Mary and Joseph appeared to be mesmerized by all of the attention Jesus was getting.

After a considerable amount of time on their knees, worshipping Jesus, they began to open the gifts they brought with them.

Everyone watching was awestruck as they presented the gifts of gold, frankincense, and myrrh to Mary and Joseph.

The crowd of people eventually began to disperse, but once again I felt drawn to the scene that was unfolding before me. I was so intrigued, I hung around to listen as the Maji began telling their story to Mary and Joseph.

I listened as the wise men talked more in depth about how their studies of the scriptures, and how the star that suddenly appeared caused them to leave their families, their businesses and travel for several months in search of the Messiah.

"How did you know to follow the star?" Joseph asked.

"Well, as Maji, we study a lot of different things, including astronomy," one of the wise men responded. "So, when this star *just appeared...* we just knew that it had a special purpose."

I listened intently as they continued talking in depth about the various prophesies that were written about the birth of Jesus.

"I know you followed the star, but how did you end up *right here* in Bethlehem?" Joseph asked.

Again, the lead Maji took charge in answering the question. "Here, let me show you something," he answered as he pulled several scrolls from his belongings.

"Here is what the prophet Micah wrote." Then he began to read... [1]*"But you, Bethlehem Ephrathah, though you are little among the thousands of Judah, yet out of you shall come forth to Me the One to be Ruler in Israel, whose goings forth are from of old, from everlasting."*

"Did you see it? It says right there that the Ruler in Israel would come out of Bethlehem."

Joseph nodded his head intently. "What other prophesies have you studied?"

"Well... let me ask you a question," he responded. "Is there any way you are a descendant of King David?"

"You bet I am... and I'm proud of it!" Joseph shouted, thumping his chest with his fist.

The old Maji grinned and flipped through another scroll. "Well, listen to what Isaiah wrote." [2]*"For unto us a Child is born, unto us a Son is given; and the government will be upon His shoulder. And His name will be called Wonderful, Counselor, Mighty God, Everlasting Father, Prince of Peace. Of the increase of His government and peace there will be no end, upon the throne of David..."*

The wise man paused and looked at Joseph. "Did you catch that 'throne of David' part?"

Joseph nodded his head, and the wise man continued reading,

²*"And over His kingdom, to order it and establish it with judgment and justice from that time forward, even forever. The zeal of the Lord of hosts will perform this.*

When he finished reading, there was complete silence as everyone looked at each other, soaking in what had just been read.

Finally, Mary quietly broke the silence as she said softly, "I quoted part of that to Joseph earlier. I told him about the *'wonderful'* part."

Again, there was a reverent silence.

"May I pick Him up?" the old Maji asked softly, nodding his head toward Jesus.

"Of course, you can," Mary answered.

The elderly wise man carefully took Jesus from Mary's arms and bowed to his knees, holding baby Jesus up toward the *star* that was shining down like a beacon from heaven.

His shoulders began trembling as he began to weep.

I watched in complete amazement as all of the other wise men, and even Joseph bowed with him.

"Men, we must never forget what is happening here. What I am holding in my hands is 'The Child', and 'The Son' that Isaiah told us would come," He sobbed.

Continuing to hold Jesus up, he continued, saying softly, *"Behold the Mighty God! Behold the everlasting Father! Behold the Prince of*

Peace!"

Then he repeated it, over and over, each time getting louder and louder.

"Behold the Mighty God! Behold the everlasting Father! Behold the Prince of Peace!"

"Behold the Mighty God! Behold the everlasting Father! Behold the Prince of Peace!"

Then each one of them raised their faces to the heavens as they shouted one last time in unison, ...

"Behold the Mighty God! Behold the everlasting Father! Behold the Prince of Peace!"

Then it grew silent again.

For the longest time it was like no one dared move or say a word.

It was clear these Maji were indeed very wise when it came to understanding the prophetic words in the sacred scrolls.

Then, breaking the silence, one of the wise men asked hesitantly, "Mary, may I ask one last, and rather personal question?"

"Well... that depends on the question. What do you want to know?" she responded, looking at Joseph with a sideways look in her eyes.

The wise man reached over and picked up the scroll and said softly, "In Isaiah's writings he also wrote that the Messiah would be born of a virgin." He then began to read, *3"Therefore the Lord Himself will give you a sign: Behold, the virgin shall conceive and bear a Son, and shall call His name Immanuel."*

"With all respect Mary... were you a virgin?"

It got very quiet.

Everyone's attention was now on Mary, and I found myself leaning in to hear her answer.

"Yes. Yes, I was… and still am, a virgin!" Mary answered emphatically, hiding a big grin behind her hand.

Joseph grinned as the jaws of each wise man dropped!

"Then that settles it!" The older wise man shouted, leaping to his feet. "This Child is without doubt… *'Emmanuel… God with us'*!!!"

Mary and Joseph just looked at each other and smiled.

Again, I was amazed at how undignified these Magi appeared as they responded. They were hooting and hollering, jumping up and down, and dancing around, slapping each other on the back.

Eventually they settled down, but they still had the biggest of grins on their faces.

UNTIL… the Maji started talking about how they had stopped in Jerusalem to see if King Herod knew about Jesus.

They told Mary and Joseph that while seeking Jesus and talking to King Herod, they had called Jesus the *"King of the Jews"* and how they quickly realized it was a big mistake. They said that King Herod was not happy with the thought of someone else being called the *"King of the Jews!"*

As soon as they shared what had happened, I saw a look of concern quickly appear on Joseph's face.

"What did Herod say?" Joseph asked, clearly distressed at what he was hearing.

"Herod said that if we found the Child to be sure and let him know, so that he could also come and worship the Child," one of the wise men answered.

"But... we knew he was lying," added another one of the wise men.

I listened intently as they told Mary and Joseph they had decided to return home a different way than the way they had come, because they didn't want to go through Jerusalem and take the chance of running into King Herod. They said they were fearful of what Herod might do if he found baby Jesus!

Again, I saw that the same way the shepherds had been hesitant to leave, the wise men also did not want to leave.

The wise men told Mary and Joseph they were going to take a day to rest at our inn before starting their long journey back home, but they repeatedly thanked Mary and Joseph for their hospitality and allowing them the privilege of meeting the Christ Child.

As soon as the Maji left, Mary and Joseph began quickly packing up their things. I could see they were anxious to leave as well.

I was so sad to see them go. By this time, I had developed a wonderful relationship with them.

"Do you have to go?" I asked, sadly.

"Yes," Joseph responded.

Joseph then shared with me what the angel had warned him about in a dream, and how King Herod was looking for Jesus so that he could kill Him.

"So instead of going back to Nazareth we're going to go to Egypt for a little while," he stated.

I was so sad to see them go. And it wasn't just because of the excitement of the visits from the shepherds and the wise men. I really liked having Jesus there. There was just something about being near Him that moved my spirit.

I hugged Mary and Joseph, and kissed baby Jesus on the forehead, not realizing it would be many years before I would see Him again.

I told them if they were ever in the neighborhood again to be sure to stop in and see us.

They repeatedly thanked me for helping them. As Mary gave me one last big hug, she held me close and prayed the most wonderful prayer of protection and blessing over me and our family.

They assured me that they would stop in if they were ever close by. They then made their way slowly on down the road toward Jerusalem. They still had to register for the census, and I knew they were fearful of being discovered by King Herod.

I sadly and quietly prayed my own prayer of protection over them as I held baby Jesus while Joseph helped Mary climb aboard their donkey. Tears were in my eyes as I handed baby Jesus to Mary.

As they began their travels, I watched them intently until they were nothing more than a dot on the horizon.

---

[1]Micah 5:2
[2]Isaiah 9:6-7
[3]Isaiah 7:14

40

CHAPTER SEVEN

As soon as I returned to the inn my father called the whole family together. We all sat in a circle around him. In his hands, he held the family copy of a scroll that contained the writings from some of the prophets.

The only other time I saw my dad this emotional was when Timothy was born.

"Are you going to read from the scrolls?" I asked.

Blinking back the emotion that was in his eyes, he answered, "yes, I am going to read some of the prophetic scriptures concerning the birth of the Messiah."

"Cool," I responded. "The Maji were just showing Mary and Joseph what the scrolls said about the Messiah."

He cleared his throat, looked at each of us in the eye, and said, "Kids, what we witnessed at our Inn the last few days is something very, very special. Our forefathers dreamed about and looked forward to this day for a long time. I remember my grandparents talking about the coming of the Messiah, but they died before they were able to see it. Since I was a child, my mom and dad frequently talked about the coming of the Messiah. They also died before they were able to see it. I can hardly believe that it has happened... and even more unbelievable is that *He was born right here at our Inn and we got to witness it!!!*"

"So, you *do* believe that Jesus is the Messiah?" I asked.

"Well, let me read what Isaiah said would happen, and then you tell me what *you* think," my dad said, as he unrolled the scroll.

He held the scroll in his hands respectfully, as if he was holding the most precious thing in the world, and softly he began to read.

[1]*"Therefore, the Lord Himself shall give you a sign. The virgin will be with child and will give birth to a Son, and you will call His name Emmanuel."*

I jumped to my feet, in excitement. *"That's exactly what one of the Magi asked Mary!!!"*

"What?" my dad asked. "What are you talking about?"

"I was listening to the wise men talking to Mary and Joseph, and that was the last question one of them asked Mary. He asked her if she was a virgin."

"He actually asked her that?" my mom questioned, with her eyebrows raised. "And pray tell, what did she say?"

"She said, *"Yes. Yes, I was... and still am, a virgin."*

"What's a virgin?" my youngest sister asked.

My dad grinned, but my mom responded, "Never mind," ignoring my sister. "How did the wise men respond to her answer?"

"They went *CRAZY!* They were jumping and dancing all over the place!!!"

My mom and dad were both stunned. They looked at each other and then began laughing as hard as they could.

"Is there more in the scroll?" I asked.

"There sure is," my dad answered, picking up the scroll again. "Let me read more of what Isaiah wrote about the Messiah."

[2]"The people walking in darkness have seen a great light; on those living in the land of the shadow of death a light has dawned. You have enlarged the nation and increased their joy; they rejoice before you as people rejoice at harvest, as men rejoice when dividing the plunder. For as in the day of Midian's defeat, you have shattered the yoke that burdens them, the bar across their shoulders; the rod of their oppressor. Every warrior's boot used in battle and every garment rolled in blood will be destined for burning, will be destined for the fire."

"Bartholomew, do you understand what that means?" my dad asked.

"It sounds like someone was having a difficult time, but things are about to get much better," I answered.

"You're right, Bartholomew. The people *'walking in darkness and living in the shadow of death'* are us, the Jewish people. We are living in the darkness, and under the yoke of the Roman government," my dad explained.

"But... listen to this," my dad continued, "listen to the promise."

Then he continued reading.

[3]"For unto us a Child is born, and unto us a Son is given..."

Immediately I cut my dad off again, "they read this one too! But go ahead... I'd like to hear it again!"

[3]"For unto us a Child is born," my dad started again. *"And unto us a Son is given; and the government will be on His shoulders. And He will be called Wonderful, Counselor, Mighty God, Everlasting Father, and Prince of Peace. Of the increase of His government and peace there will be no end. He will reign on David's throne and over his kingdom, establishing and upholding it with justice and righteousness from that time on and forever. The zeal of the Lord Almighty will accomplish this."*

The same thing happened to us that happened to the wise men. I remember the solemn hush that fell over us as soon as my dad finished reading.

My dad finished by saying, "Family, we must never forget what happened here."

I also remember the few days that followed. It was like the stable where Jesus had been born was now holy ground.

---

[1]Isaiah 7:14
[2]Isaiah 9:2-5
[3]Isaiah 9:6-7

CHAPTER EIGHT

From what the Maji and Joseph said we knew that King Herod was looking for Jesus. However, we had no idea just how much he wanted to kill Him.

Looking back on it, it only made sense that King Herod would do everything he could to eliminate Jesus. Throughout history anytime a king feared someone could possibly take the throne away from him, he would have that person executed... sometimes even if that person was his own son!

The day after Mary, Joseph and Jesus left there was a knock on our front door.

Little did I know that an unbelievable nightmare was getting ready to unfold in our happy family.

When I opened the door, there stood several of King Herod's soldiers. Shoving me aside they came barging into our house shouting... *"Where is the boy? Where is the boy?"*

My dad thought they meant Jesus. "He's not here. They left yesterday," he responded.

"No... where is *YOUR* boy? Where is *TIMOTHY*?" the brute of a soldier shouted, walking up to my dad until they were nose to nose.

"My boy? Why are you asking about Timothy?" my dad answered, refusing to budge.

"By the order of King Herod, you must give him to us!"

"I don't care what King Herod said, you are *NOT* taking my son!" my dad shouted into the soldier's face, blocking the door to Timothy's room.

"Get out of my way," the solder shouted into my father's face. *"I don't have a problem with taking your life if I have to!"*

"Well, that's exactly what you're going to have to do... because I'm not letting you near my son!!!" my dad shouted back at him.

One of the other soldiers quickly pulled his sword and slammed the blunt end against the side of my father's head, instantly knocking him unconscious!

All I remember after that is charging the soldier that attacked my dad. I landed one punch squarely on the jaw of the soldier that hit my dad, and he grunted and staggered backwards. Instantly everything faded into darkness, as I felt a sharp pain in the back of my head from the blunt end of another soldier's sword.

When I woke up my mom and sisters were huddled together in front of Timothy's bedroom, screaming uncontrollably. My dad was still laying in the floor unconscious.

I shook my head, trying to clear the cobwebs that were in my mind, and crawled over to where they were.

Then I saw the worst sight I could possibly have ever imagined. There in my mother's arms was the bloody, lifeless body of Timothy!

The lights in my head went out again, and I crumpled to the floor.

I don't know how long I remained unconscious, but the next time I woke up there was nothing other than complete silence.

I rolled over and sat up, only to see my mom and dad sitting beside each other on the floor, with Timothy's lifeless and bloodied body still in my mother's arms. My sisters were huddled up against them, and everyone was quietly staring, in shock, at his tiny body, in disbelief.

My mom was rocking him back and forth, crying, *"Why??? Why??? Why???"*

This scene was replayed in every household with young boys under the age of two.

Our family, our community, was never the same.

CHAPTER NINE

The next few days were a blur.

First of all, due to Jewish tradition, Timothy had to be buried within twenty-four hours.

I don't remember very much about the funeral other than the tiny casket, lots of people telling us how sorry they were, and my entire family crying uncontrollably.

Then came the horrendous aftermath.

My mom and dad wandered around the inn like they were walking in their sleep. My sisters cried non-stop. There was this huge empty place in our lives.

I didn't know how to act. I had lost my little buddy.

For me it was a very confusing time. On one hand I remembered how wonderful it was while Mary, Joseph and Jesus were with us.

There were so many great memories.

I remembered when they first arrived and how Joseph helped me build the manger. I was so appreciative for the time he took to show me a few things about carpentry and how to use the new tools I had just received for my birthday.

I remembered how Mary and Joseph treated each other with so much love and respect.

I remembered what it felt like when Jesus grabbed my finger, and the warmth that overwhelmed my entire body!

How could I forget all of the excitement surrounding the shepherds and their stories?

How could I forget the wealthy Maji, their expensive gifts... and their exhilarating stories?

I had never felt anything that awesome in my entire life!

To then go from feeling so wonderful, to feeling like the world was collapsing around me... it was too much for my fifteen-year-old mind to comprehend.

Before King Herod's soldiers showed up, I honestly thought that those few days with Mary, Joseph, and Jesus would be some of the fondest memories I would have in my entire lifetime.
BUT NOW...???

I struggled with anger... and resentment.

I found myself blaming Mary and Joseph.

I even found myself... blaming Jesus!

I couldn't stop myself from thinking that if Jesus had never been born here, we would still have Timothy!

TIMOTHY!!!

What were we going to do without little Timothy? How were we supposed to get used to no longer hearing his bubbly voice, and the pitter patter of his small feet around the house?

I watched as my mom and dad, and all my sisters tried to come to grips with the loss of Timothy.

The heart wrenching grief also went beyond just our family. I watched as our neighbors and friends, that had also lost their little boys, struggled with trying to cope with their tragic loss as well.

The entire village of Bethlehem was overwhelmed with sorrow, mourning, and grief!

One day, by pure coincidence, I ran into the old shepherd that came to see Jesus, and Matthew, his grandson in Bethlehem. I listened in horror, as Matthew told me how the soldiers had killed his little brother, Jonathon, as well.

My heart broke, as I watched the old shepherd's shoulders shaking, as his whole body trembled beneath the heavy weight of grief. Even though it had been several months since the soldiers came, it opened those deep wounds once again, and we embraced and cried on each other's shoulders for the longest time.

Just about every family in and around Bethlehem had family members, or close friends, that had lost a small son to Herod's evil plot to eliminate the threat of Jesus becoming the *King of the Jews*.

For years, I woke up and went to sleep, to the sound of my mother weeping. For several months my father walked around like he was in a daze.

And the manger...

I had been so very proud of that manger. I had even written on the bottom of it, *"Constructed by Bartholomew and Joseph"* in big, bold letters!

Now every time I saw it, even though it was shoved to the back wall of the stable where Jesus had been born, I was conflicted. On one hand I wanted to keep it because of the wonderful memories associated with it, but on the other hand every time I saw it, it brought so much pain to my heart I could hardly stand it!

One day I heard the sound of boards being ripped apart and I walked outside to see my dad, with tears streaming down his face, tearing down the stable where Jesus had been born. That was all it took... I grabbed the hammer that I had used to build that manger and I smashed it into a thousand pieces!

My dad and I then piled all of the pieces together in a heap and stood together with our arms wrapped around each other, watching the remnants of the manger and stable burn until all that was left was a pile of ashes.

And then... *NOTHING*. We heard absolutely *NOTHING* about Jesus.

Years went by.

Oh, there was talk at every community gathering about how His birth had brought so much pain and sorrow to Bethlehem and the surrounding villages, but no one seemed to know where He was or what He was doing.

More time passed.

Eventually life went back to being as normal as it possibly could.

After several years my mom gathered the courage to go through all of Timothy's clothes and gave most of them to families in need. Even though most of Timothy's room had been cleaned out, there still seemed to be constant reminders of Timothy everywhere we turned.

Our lives had been tragically changed... forever.

And it was hard to keep from blaming Jesus!

CHAPTER TEN

It was twelve years later. I was twenty-seven years old.

I was married and had two children of my own, a little boy and a little girl. My wife and I had built a new house right next to the inn, so we could help Mom and Dad run the inn.

Life had reached a place where I was fairly happy, unless someone mentioned Timothy's name. As a family we had an unspoken agreement to remember Timothy in our own private ways, but we seldom spoke of the tragic event that led to his death.

I continued in the Jewish traditions that my parents had taught me, such as Yom Kippur, where we performed a complete fast for twenty-five hours; the Feast of Tabernacles, which lasts for seven days; and Passover, which lasts for eight days.

I raised both of my kids to memorize scripture from the Pentateuch, which are the first five books of the Scriptures, and we traveled into Jerusalem often to pray in the Temple.

Yet, all of it seemed nothing more than laws and vain repetitions.

From what I saw, the Priests and High Priests were only in it for self-gain and hypocrisy.

One day there was a knock at the front door of the inn. When I opened it... I could hardly believe my eyes. There stood Mary and Joseph!

The look on their faces was a look of sadness and desperation.

I didn't quite know how to respond, so I just stood there staring at them.

"Is that really you, Bartholomew?" Joseph asked, with hesitation in his voice.

I nodded my head *yes*... still not able to speak.

He awkwardly tried to make small talk. "My, you have really grown. You look a lot like your father."

I continued staring... not quite sure how to respond.

He continued, "Are you still using your carpenter tools to build stuff?" he asked, in an effort to break the ice.

However, I was still not ready to make amends, and continued to stare at him, unable to respond.

Realizing he was wasting his time, Joseph hung his head and said sadly, "Bartholomew, we heard what happened after we left twelve years ago. We are so very sorry about Timothy. We had no idea that King Herod would do something that horrible."

I was torn. Down deep I knew that it wasn't their fault, but the pain was still there.

"What are you doing here?" I asked curtly.

Slightly relieved that I at least responded, he continued. "We took the family to Jerusalem this year for Passover... and on our way back home we realized that Jesus wasn't with us."

I just stared at them, unblinking.

Joseph continued. "Since we were close, we thought we would stop by and see if per chance... maybe He had showed up here?"

"No... He isn't here." I responded sharply.

Even though I was feeling angry, I still felt so sorry for Mary.
54

She stood there trembling and muttering, *"What are we going to do? What are we going to do?"*

After a minute of silence, Joseph wrapped one of his arms over her shoulders and said, "Come on Mary, this is much too painful for him."

They sadly turned and started walking away, and Joseph looked back over his shoulder and said, "It's okay, Bartholomew, we understand."

However, … after only a few steps, Mary quickly turned around and ran back to me.

With tears streaming down her face she embraced me. *"Oh Bartholomew…"* she cried, *"We are SO… VERY…VERY… SORRY!"*

Then she turned and rejoined Joseph and they slowly walked away…

There was a part of me that wanted to run after her and tell her I understood that it wasn't their fault, but… I just couldn't. It felt like my lips and my feet were frozen. So, I just stood and watched as they slowly made their way on down the road.

Hearing a conversation, Naomi, my wife, came to the front door. "Who was that?" she asked.

"It was Mary and Joseph."

"*The* Mary and Joseph?"

"Yes. It was the parents of Jesus."

"What in the world did they want? Haven't they caused enough grief for this family?" she asked gruffly.

"It's okay dear. Apparently, they were on their way home from Jerusalem, and Jesus has gone missing," I answered.

"And just what, pray tell, did they want from you?" she asked, still showing a gruffness in her voice.

"They wanted to know if He had shown up here?" I replied.

Her voice softened slightly. "What did you tell them?"

"I told them He hadn't been here."

Sensing my conflict, she took me in her arms and we just stood there for the longest time.

That was the last time I saw Mary and Joseph together.

A few years later a family from Nazareth spent the night at our inn. I couldn't help but ask if they knew Mary and Joseph. They said they did. When I asked how they were doing they informed us that Joseph had passed away.

My heart went out to Mary, and I actually prayed that God would help her.

Then, once again... we heard *NOTHING about Jesus for a time.*

CHAPTER ELEVEN

Years passed. My son and daughter grew into their teen years. Mom and Dad were getting older and having a difficult time with their age and health, so Naomi and I pretty much ran the inn ourselves.

When my son turned fifteen, I gave him his own set of carpenter tools, the same way my dad had done for me. Every time I showed my son some of the carpenter tricks I had learned over the years, my mind went back to that night Joseph and I built that manger. I found myself wishing I had been more forgiving that day, years ago, when Jesus was missing.

My heart was starting to heal.

From time to time my dad and I would sit down and talk about what might have happened to Jesus. If He truly was the Messiah, as the shepherds and wise men had said, (and even as we thought at the time...) why hadn't we heard anything about Him?

The political climate was still the same because the Romans were still in charge. The king that had Timothy put to death, had died, however, his son was now sitting on the throne. Things for the Jews were still as bad as they had ever been.

Then... before I realized it, another 18 years passed.

At least four or five times a year I would travel into Jerusalem to purchase supplies for the inn. Three years ago, while on one of those trips, the shop keeper I frequently bought supplies from asked if I had heard the latest news.

I said, "I guess not... what is the latest news?"

He said, "Do you remember about thirty years ago when the previous King Herod had all those little boys killed?"

Suddenly, out of the blue, all of those horrible feelings came flooding back. In my mind I could see Herod's soldiers attacking my dad, and then attacking me. The sight of my sisters gathered around my mom and dad, and Timothy's small, lifeless and bloody body in my mother's arms, came roaring back with a vengeance.

"Yes... I remember that... *VERY WELL*..." I answered, a little surprised at the emotion that quickly came to my voice. *"My little brother was one of those little boys!"*

"Oh... I'm sorry," the shop keeper replied apologetically, "but that baby boy that caused all that ruckus is back in town."

"What??? Jesus is here in Jerusalem?" I asked.

"Yes! And rumor has it that He has some kind of ability to heal sick people and perform all kinds of miracles!"

"Really? Have you seen Him?"

"No, but I heard He turned water into wine at a wedding in Cana."

"Well," that's not much of a miracle. It sounds more like a magic trick," I said, with a little bit of skepticism in my voice.

"He then supposedly healed a little boy in Capernaum that was about to die."

That story definitely got my attention, as my thoughts went back to little Timothy once again.

"And," the shop keeper continued, "they say He also cast a demonic spirit out of a man in Capernaum!"

I didn't quite know how to respond, so I just finished loading up my goods and started back home.

I don't mind telling you, my mind was in a whirlwind the entire trip back home to Bethlehem.

Should I say anything to my elderly parents?
Should I say anything to my sisters?

I decided to keep it to myself for a little while. There was no need in opening old wounds if I didn't have to.

But afterwards, every time I would travel into Jerusalem to purchase supplies, that same shop keeper had more and more stories.

A story about Jesus helping some fishermen miraculously catch so many fish that it filled two boatloads!

A story about how Jesus was healing LEPERS!

Stories that Jesus had healed a couple of men that everyone knew were truly paralyzed!

And... a story about Jesus healing a man with a withered hand!

However... the story that really got my attention was the story the inn keeper told me about Jesus raising a widow woman's son from the dead in Nain.

"He actually raised a little boy from the dead?" I asked. "And there was no doubt the boy was dead?"

"Oh, he was dead alright. The family had already had the funeral and they were carrying the casket to the graveyard when Jesus stopped the funeral procession and reached out and touched the casket. They say all He said was, 'Young man, I say to you, get up!' And the boy immediately came back to life, sat up, and started talking to his mother!"

I was flabbergasted! As hard as I tried, I could not stop the memory of *my family* carrying Timothy's little casket to the cemetery, and *my mom* barely able to walk due to the enormous amount of grief she was carrying.

To find out that when Jesus encountered a mother going through what my mom went through, He actually raised her son from the dead... that was most definitely causing a change in my feelings about Jesus.

I finally decided it was time to tell my dad the stories I was hearing.

It was the strangest conversation. Both of us were conflicted.

On one hand we wanted to check it out to see if it was true. Was Jesus the Messiah? Was He going to deliver us from the Romans? On one hand we wanted to go into Jerusalem and track Him down and see for ourselves... but on the other hand the memory of Timothy held us back.

We decided to call a family meeting and tell the whole family what I had been hearing. There were mixed feelings. My two younger sisters were more willing to check it out, but my parents and two older sisters were still not quite sure.

I continued my trips into Jerusalem, and I have to admit I was becoming more and more curious about what was going on with Jesus. I looked forward to finding out the latest miracle from my shop keeper friend.

"You'll never believe what He did just a couple of weeks ago," he stated. "Do you remember that big storm that blew up, seemingly out of nowhere?"

"I sure do. I was out in the field mending a fence and the sky got so dark and the wind blew up so quickly, and violently I actually feared for my life. And then, something happened I have never seen before. It normally takes a long time for a storm that violent to calm back down, but that day it happened instantly!"

"Jesus did that!"

"Seriously? How?" I asked, in amazement.

"He was out in a boat with His disciples when that storm blew in, and according to the disciples He simply spoke to the wind and waves and they obeyed His voice!"

I just stood there looking at him in disbelief.

"However... that's not the best news I have for you. I remember how touched you were when Jesus raised that little boy from the dead. Guess what?" he asked, with a big grin on his face.

"Did He do it again???"

"He sure did. This time it was a little girl. Have you been to the synagogue?"

"Of course, I have... many, many times."

"Have you ever met Jairus, one of the Synagogue rulers?"

"I sure have," I said. "His daughter is the same age as my granddaughter."

Then it hit me... *"NO... not HIS daughter???"* I asked in disbelief.

My friend shook his head up and down. *"Yes... it was his daughter!"*

I couldn't move for a few seconds.

"Seriously," I continued, "on one of our trips to the Synagogue my granddaughter went with us, and she and his daughter met and played together. She was the sweetest child!"

My mind was spinning. "And... she is the one that died?"

"Yep!"

"But... Jesus raised her from the dead???"

"Yep!!!"

Once more I went back home, more excited than ever to share what I had heard.

This time my family was much more receptive to my stories about Jesus, especially my daughter.

Then, several months ago I had to go to Bethsaida on a business trip. As I was walking down the main street a young lad came running out of one of the merchant's shops with a small bag in his hand, almost knocking me down.

"Hey! Watch where you're going!" I shouted at him.

"Oh, I'm so sorry sir, but I'm in a hurry," the lad responded breathlessly, "there's a big crowd following Jesus and I'm going to go check it out. I thought I'd better take a sack lunch with me since no one seems to know how long we're going to be gone. I hear He performs all kinds of miracles and I want to see for myself!"

He was so excited and talking so fast I could barely keep up with what he said.

"Did you say *Jesus*?"

"Yes."

"And... you say it's the same Jesus that's supposedly been performing all kinds of miracles?"

"Yes. I'm sorry sir, but I need to run. I don't want to miss it."

"And... He's here in Bethsaida?" I asked excitedly.

"Yes, He's right outside the city, heading toward the mountains."

The lad then paused. "Hey, do you want to go with me?"

I hesitated, but then made a quick decision. *"Why not?"* I answered. *"I've been wanting to check Him out too!"*

It was all I could do to keep up with the young lad, but I managed to keep him in sight until we caught up with the multitude of people that were heading out of town.

I decided to keep a low profile, so I stayed toward the back of the crowd. The last time I saw the young lad he was working his way to the front of the multitude.

We finally reached a place where thousands of people were being seated on the side of the mountain, so they could see and hear Jesus below us.

I sat there listening as the voice of Jesus echoed up to where I was sitting. His voice was so clear and strong. He spoke with such authority I was mesmerized. He spoke about a *"kingdom of heaven"*. I couldn't take my eyes off of Him!

Even though there were at least five or six thousand people there, I was amazed at how quiet and reverent everyone was. All I could think was, *"This must be what Michael the archangel's voice sounds like!"*

After several hours the multitude started getting restless. But before people started leaving, I saw Jesus call several of His disciples together. The disciples then spread out and started separating everyone into groups of fifty.

All around me I started hearing whispers... *"What's going on? What is He getting ready to do? Is He going to perform some kind of miracle?"*

Then I sensed it. *"Yes... He is getting ready to do something miraculous!"*

I caught sight of the young lad that almost knocked me down. Jesus was holding his small sack of food. *"Is He going to eat that young man's lunch right here in front of everyone?"* I wondered. *"That would just be rude!"*

Instead, the multitude watched as Jesus bowed His head and prayed, and then reached into the sack and brought out a small loaf of bread and began breaking it into pieces and handing it to the disciples.

I couldn't believe my eyes! Over and over He reached into the sack and brought out more and more bread! Thousands and thousands of pieces of bread!

Then... He reached into the small bag and started bringing out fish! Handfuls of fish! Over and over, He reached into the bag and brought out thousands of fish!

People around me were standing, and pointing, and laughing. It was the most amazing sight I had ever seen!

However, the craziest thing was... after it was over, there were so many leftovers the twelve disciples came around with baskets and every basket was overflowing with leftovers. Twelve baskets full of leftovers! And it all started with a small sack lunch! If I hadn't seen it with my own eyes, I would never have believed it!

I could hardly wait to get back home to tell my family what I had witnessed. It took quite some time to convince them that I was telling the truth!

I don't mind telling you, my mind was in a whirlwind. Should I go try to find Jesus and find out more? I remembered how excited I was when Jesus was born, and then how devastated and disappointed I was when Timothy was killed. If I opened my heart and mind to

Jesus, would it end the same way it did the first time?

I questioned every traveler that stopped at our inn to see if they had heard anything about Jesus. More and more stories were being told.

One story was about a man named Lazarus that had been dead for four days. Supposedly after being dead for *four days*, Jesus raised him from the dead!

Now my entire family was asking anyone returning from Jerusalem if they had any stories about Jesus.

The entire family was healing!

CHAPTER TWELVE

Knowing that the time for Passover was getting closer I called the family together to see if they wanted to go and celebrate in Jerusalem. Everyone agreed, so the whole family, including my siblings and their families, packed up enough supplies to stay for several days.

When we got there, the city of Jerusalem was absolutely packed with people. Hundreds of thousands of people were there to celebrate what was considered our most important Holy Day.

My family was excited about Passover, but everyone was even more excited at the possibility of seeing Jesus and witnessing Him perform a miracle first-hand.

We were having a wonderful time as the streets were filled with music and celebrations, until we saw an angry throng of people marching down the street toward us.

They were on the road that leads toward the hill called Calvary.

Then we heard them chanting something awful... *"CRUCIFY HIM... CRUCIFY HIM..."*

The crowd in the street parted as the throng made their way past us.

Then I saw Him.

There in the center of that throng of people was a man with a cross on His back. He had been beaten so severely and was covered with so much blood He was un-recognizable.

I leaned over to the man standing next to me and asked, *"Who is that Man?"*

"You must not be from Jerusalem. That is JESUS CHRIST!!!" he answered.

"THAT... is Jesus Christ??? The same Jesus that has been performing miracles?"

I could not believe my eyes. I was very confused.

Again, I leaned over and asked, *"Why is He being crucified?"*

"He claims He is the Son of God. He is being crucified for blasphemy."

Like a flood... the memories of 33 years ago came pouring back into my mind!

I remembered the Shepherds, and how they showed up specifically looking for a babe wrapped in swaddling clothes, lying in a manger.

I remembered how excited they were at the thought of seeing Jesus.

I remembered how there was absolutely no way those shepherds could have known that Jesus was at our inn, unless the angels showed them the way and had indeed told them that Jesus was the Savior... that He was, undeniably, *CHRIST THE LORD!*

I remembered the wise men, and the amazing gifts they brought with them. I remembered the stories they shared with us about how they had followed that star for months. How that star led them right to the very stable that was on our property. And how they were so convinced that baby Jesus was, without doubt, the Messiah!

Like a flood, the memory came rushing back into my mind of my dad calling the whole family together, and us listening so intently as he excitedly read from the writings of Isaiah concerning the virgin birth!

Now, suddenly, I realized what I had known deep in my heart all along... YES... that baby born in our stable was, beyond the shadow of a doubt... ***THE MESSIAH!***

68

Yes, Jesus Christ was indeed the **SAVIOR OF THE WORLD!**

But, why was He now being led to His death?

I had so many questions.

I turned to my family and told them to go back home to Bethlehem. However, I told my dad that felt like I just *had* to stay. I *had* to see what was going to happen.

So, I followed the crowd.

I watched as Jesus stumbled beneath the cross, and the soldiers forced a man from the crowd to help Him.

I listened as the Pharisees and Sadducees hurled disgusting insults at Him. Yet, not one time did He respond. He kept His head bowed and never spoke a word.

I watched, and followed, until we reached the place that was called *"The Skull"* or... Golgotha.

Then, as if the beating He had taken wasn't enough humiliation, they ripped His clothes from His bloodied body, leaving Him naked. They laughed, mockingly, as they gambled over who would get His garment.

Then, I could hardly believe my eyes as I watched as Jesus willingly lay down on that cross.

"Why isn't He fighting? Why isn't He trying to get away?" I wondered.

I watched as a cold-hearted Roman soldier steadied the spike of a nail onto Jesus' palm with one hand, while he raised the hammer he held in his opposite hand, preparing to pierce His flesh. And I winced as he drove that nail into the hand of Jesus with a sickening *thud*!

The pain and agony on the face of Jesus was so awful, He no longer looked human, as the soldier completed the task of driving the nail into His hand.

I winced again, as the same soldier placed a second nail on the other hand, and again raised the hammer... and with another sickening *thud* drove the nail into that hand just like the first!

The cry that came from Jesus was heart wrenching, as again and again the hammer was raised and came crashing down with another sickening *thud*!

It was almost more than I could bear to watch as the soldier crossed Jesus' feet and once more raised the hammer and drove an even larger nail into His feet. Over and over the sickening thud reverberated through the stillness that now surrounded the scene.

The once rowdy crowd had suddenly gone silent. Gone were the chants. Now no one was laughing.

My mind went numb, as they raised the cross into the air, and it dropped with another sickening 'thud' into the hole prepared in the ground.

"Why??? Why??? Why would they be treating Jesus this way. Why didn't someone come to His defense? Where were the thousands of people that He had healed?"

As I stood there in the eerie stillness, my mind went back to the stable... and the manger. I watched those fingers, that were now reaching toward the nails in an attempt to ease the pain, and I remember those tiny fingers wrapped around mine.

The words the wise men spoke, *The King Of The Jews,* took on a different meaning as I looked at the crown of thorns that had been crushed down upon His brow. I remembered kissing that forehead and ruffling His dark, curly hair that was now matted and soaked with clotting blood.

I remembered how in awe I was, and the amazement I felt, while I watched the shepherds and the wise men bow, overcome with emotion, as they worshipped baby Jesus.

Then I saw it. The sign. The sign that had been nailed above His head. There, written in Greek, Latin, and Hebrew, were the words... *"This Is The King Of The Jews."*

Again, my mind went back to the conversation I heard the wise men have with Mary and Joseph, as they talked in hush tones about how King Herod was so upset that Jesus was being called *"The King Of The Jews."*

I wasn't sure how all of this was going to end up, but I knew I couldn't leave.

And then... there at the foot of the cross I saw her. MARY!!! Sweet... Precious... Mary. And my heart broke.

She was laying at the foot of the cross, with the disciple named John by her side, sobbing uncontrollably. The anguish and pain on her face was overwhelming.

Like a tidal wave it hit me. She was losing her Son, the same way my mom and dad had lost their son!

She was feeling the same agony that our whole family felt when Timothy was so brutally taken from us.

I stayed until the very end. *I simply could not leave.*

I stayed until I heard Jesus ask God to forgive those that were crucifying Him. I stayed until I saw His head fall to His chest, as He took His last breath.

Then all doubt of who He was, was erased.

Even though it was only three o'clock in the afternoon, the sky suddenly turned dark as midnight! The earth began quaking beneath my feet! I watched as huge boulders split in two!

I thought for a second that the wrath of God was being poured out, and we were all going to be destroyed.

Through the darkness I heard the Roman soldier shout out, **"TRULY THIS WAS THE SON OF GOD!"**

All doubt was gone. *"Yes..."* I said to myself. *"Jesus truly was The Son of God!"*

"Now what??? It wasn't supposed to end this way, was it???"

Eventually the darkness lifted, and the crowd slowly began to leave. But I just couldn't move.

A soldier approached Jesus' body with a long spear in his hand. *"Now what?"* I thought. *"Haven't they mutilated His body enough?"*

Then I realized what he was doing. He was checking to make sure Jesus really was dead, as he plunged the spear into Jesus' side. Out came what looked like blood mixed with water.

Now, the only ones left were Mary, John, and a few other women.

Still at a distance I watched as one of the disciples finally came, and tenderly took down His body, and carried Him away.

I lingered, unwilling to go back home. Something told me to stay.

CHAPTER THIRTEEN

For three days I hung around Jerusalem… not sure of what I was waiting for.

I went to the temple, to see if anyone there knew what was going on, but the priests appeared to be as confused as everyone else. I overheard them arguing over what caused the veil in the temple to rip from top to bottom. So, I realized they weren't going to be any help.

I asked several people on the streets if anyone knew where Mary and the disciples were, but it appeared they had all gone into hiding. Considering what had just happened to Jesus, I didn't blame them.

I still couldn't bring myself to leave. *Something* told me to stay.

I went back to Mount Calvary, and sat there for two days, trying to make sense of what I had witnessed.

Three days later, I decided it was time to go back home, so I got up early in the morning, packed up my belongings, and started to leave Jerusalem.

I stopped by a small shop to get something to eat for breakfast when a young man came running past the shop, yelling as loudly as he could… ***"HE'S ALIVE! HE'S ALIVE!"***

I looked at the shop owner, and several of those seated at tables around me, and it was like everyone realized what the young man meant at the same time!

JESUS WAS ALIVE!!! HE HAD BEEN RESURRECTED FROM THE DEAD!!!

I left my half-eaten breakfast and started scurrying down the street, stopping every person I ran into. *"Have you heard anything about Jesus?"*

Throughout the day more and more stories were being told. Stories about how He had appeared to His disciples! Stories about how He had appeared to two people on the road to Emmaus! Stories that the nail prints were still in His hands and His feet! Hundreds of people were confirming that IT WAS TRUE! JESUS WAS ALIVE!!!

And I KNEW... I KNEW it was TRUE...
I just KNEW... that it was TRUE!!!

CHAPTER FOURTEEN

It's been fifty days since Jesus was raised from the dead!

Once again, I had the difficult task of convincing my family of what I had seen and heard. They finally believed me when I told them what time the sky had darkened and the earth had quaked, because they saw and heard the same thing at the same time!

Things I had been taught were now starting to fall into place.

Now, all of the Holy Days had more significance.

My dad sat down with the whole family and read more scriptures from Isaiah, as we started putting the pieces together.

We started to realize that Jesus represented the lambs that were slain in the temple for our sins! Passover has a whole new meaning. We started to understand that when we apply the blood of Jesus Christ to the door posts of our lives, the curse of death passes over us!

We started to realize that Jesus didn't come to set us free from the Roman government. He came to set us from the bondage of sin!

I convinced the whole family to make one more trip with me to Jerusalem.

This morning, my mom, my dad, and all of my sisters and their families went to Jerusalem with me to celebrate The Day of Pentecost.

Once again, the city was full of people from a lot of different countries.

What happened next can only be explained as divine providence. I can only attribute it to God allowing us to be in the right place at the right time.

We were walking near a place called the *Upper Room* when we heard a loud disturbance, so we went to see what was going on.

We watched as over a hundred people came pouring out of that Upper Room. The strangest thing was happening. They were speaking in all kinds of different languages!

I turned to my wife and told her, *"I'm not sure what's going on here, but I know this… these people are speaking languages that I'm sure they shouldn't know how to speak!"*

Realizing the same thing, my dad grabbed me by the arm and with a weird look on his face he asked, *"How in the world do these people know all these languages? These aren't foreigners. They're just a bunch of common people from right here in Galilee!"*

Again, by divine providence, I witnessed all around us, people from countries that spoke the languages we were hearing. They were totally amazed as well.

Then I saw her. MARY!!! The mother of Jesus!!!

The last time I saw her she was kneeling at the foot of the cross, weeping as though her whole life was completely shattered. But now, her face was lit up like that of an angel, as she stood there with her hands lifted to heaven, speaking in what sounded like the most heavenly language.

I ran as quickly as I could. Pushing and shoving people out of the way, until I was there in front of her.

Finally, she opened her eyes. Our eyes met!

"Bartholomew!!!" She shouted.

Thirty-three years of anger, pain, frustration, and questions were all washed away in an instant as we fell into each other's arms.

She took my face in her hands, and asked, "Do you believe? Do you believe that that little baby that was born in your stable is the Son of God?"

"YES!" I shouted at the top of my lungs. "I BELIEVE!!!"

By this time my entire family had gathered around Mary. We had a wonderful time of forgiveness and celebration!

CHAPTER FIFTEEN

"They're drunk!" several people around us began shouting, trying to explain the strange phenomenon that was going on.

"Look at 'em. This whole bunch is drunk. They should be arrested!"

Then, what appeared to be the leader of the group, named Peter, stood up and began speaking.

He said, *"These people aren't drunk. Look, it's only nine o'clock in the morning."*

Now that he had everyone's attention, he went on to explain how these people were able to speak in a language they didn't know.

He quoted from the book of Joel about how God would pour out His Spirit, and how sons and daughters would prophecy, and how old men would dream dreams.

He made it very clear that anyone and everyone that called on the name of the Lord would be saved.

I was mesmerized. I had never heard anything like this in my entire life!

He continued preaching about Jesus, and how He performed miracles, and signs and wonders. He told everyone how the Pharisee's handed Jesus over to be put to death by nailing Him to the cross. *"But,"* Peter shouted at the top of his voice, *"God raised Him from the dead!"*

When he made that statement, the whole crowd got very, very quiet, just waiting to hear what he would say next!

I listened in amazement as Peter clearly laid out how God had not only raised Jesus from the dead, but how Jesus had been exalted to the right hand of God, and how the promise of the Holy Spirit had been poured out right there in front of us.

Realizing they were guilty, several men around me, shouted out, *"What must we do?"*

"You must repent, and every one of you must be baptized in the name of Jesus Christ for the remission of your sins... and you shall receive the gift of the Holy Spirit."

I turned to my family and said, "I think we need to do what this guy is telling us to do!"

Mary stepped up and said, *"Yes... Yes... Yes... You need to do exactly what Peter just told you!"*

We were part of the three thousand people that accepted Jesus Christ as their Lord and Savior that day.

My entire family got saved and baptized today...

Including my ten-year grandson who we named TIMOTHY!!!

EPILOGUE

You see it doesn't matter if you're the owner of an Inn...

It doesn't matter if you're a lowly shepherd, or an educated wise man...

It doesn't even matter if you're a fifteen-year-old boy who cleans out stables...

Everyone that comes in contact with Jesus The Christ has their own story to tell.

Some stories may include extreme sorrow, grief, and challenges, just like Bartholomew and his family. But as long as Jesus is part of your story, in the end your story finishes well!

Tell YOUR story!!!

Other books by Steve E. Upchurch
The Adventures of Matthew and Andy: Genesis
The Adventures of Matthew and Andy: Exodus – Joshua
The Adventures of Matthew and Andy: Judges – 2 Samuel
With more on the way!

Matthew is a ten-year-old boy that has had a hard time reading and understanding his Bible. He prays and asks God to help him, and God sends a short, stocky, red-headed, freckle faced angel (named Andy) to visit Matthew in his dreams. The quirky angel has short stubby wings, and wears a #23 basketball jersey, gym shorts, and tennis shoes!

In Matthew's dreams, Andy takes Matthew back in time to see first-hand just how exciting the stories in the Bible can be! In books #2 and #3 they are joined by Pete the Parrot, and Dorcus the Donkey. Each Bible adventure is described with it's exciting twists and turns as seen through the eyes and mind of ten-year-old Matthew.

Books may be ordered at:
Steve E. Upchurch's Facebook page
E-mail: Steveup93@hotmail.com
Website: Steveup93@wixsite.com
By calling or texting 618.780.7564
or
Online at Amazon.com or Barnes & Noble
Nook & Kindle versions are also available.
This series of books is appropriate for kids from 8-12 years old.

ACKNOWLEDGEMENTS:

First and foremost, all glory, honor, and credit to my Lord and Savior Jesus Christ. The Lord has watched me, protected me, and shown me favor my entire life. He has blessed me more than I could ever have deserved. In the words of my dad, Charles Upchurch, *"All that I have, that I count dear, I owe to the Lord!"*

To my beautiful wife, Jennifer Upchurch: God saw exactly what I needed and sent you into my life. You are my love, my best friend, my help mate in ministry, and now one of my editors! I don't know what I'd do without you. I love you with all of my heart!

To my lovely children, Heather (and Jason) Roesch, Kyle Upchurch, and Zachary Brandt: I am proud of each and every one of you. I could not ask for a more wonderful family. You make my heart happy!

To my wonderful granddaughter, Jaylyn Roesch: You are an absolute delight. I can't wait to see how God uses you in His kingdom!

To my Godly parents, Charles and Mildred Upchurch: Thank you for introducing me to Jesus Christ. Thank you for a great example of what a Godly marriage should look like. Thank you for teaching me the value of hard work. And thank you for five wonderful siblings.

To my five amazing siblings, Judy (and William) Swindle, Roy (and Kathy) Upchurch, Fay (and Albert/O.J.) Suarez, Joy (and Bill) Rutherford, and Melody (and Fred) Albanito: Thank you for so many wonderful birthdays, Thanksgivings, Christmas', and family reunions. I am blessed beyond measure!

To the Staff at The Rock Church of Centralia, Illinois: Stephanie Murphy (Children's Pastor), Rod Diel (Worship Pastor), Matt Shook (Youth Pastor), Scott Becker (Church Administrator), Logan Anderson (Graphics & Media Director) and Kathy Branson (Custodian). Thank you for all of the hard work that goes into ministering to the sheep God has called us to take care of. Each and every one of you are amazing!

To the members of The Rock Church of Centralia, Illinois: Thank you for allowing me to be your pastor. It is an honor and privilege to be your local shepherd. Let's keep doing what God has called us to do until we get out of here!!!

To Crystal Deeds: Thank you so very much for your expertise in self-publishing and editing!
To Jim Shain: Thank you so very much for your expertise in editing and punctuation!

www.ingramcontent.com/pod-product-compliance
Lightning Source LLC
Chambersburg PA
CBHW072017170626
46813CB00005B/2174